Nighty-Night, Cooper

For Mary Wilcox—with lots and lots of thanks. —L.N.

For my friend Barry's grandson, Jonah Eli Beck. —L.M.

Text copyright © 2013 Laura Numeroff
Illustrations copyright © 2013 by Lynn Munsinger

HMH Books is an imprint of Houghton Mifflin Harcourt Publishing Company.

www.hmhbooks.com

The text of this book is set in Adobe Garamond.

Library of Congress Cataloging-in-Publication Data
Numeroff, Laura Joffe.
Nighty-night, Cooper / [text by Laura Numeroff ; illustrations by Lynn Munsinger].
p. cm.
Summary: It is bedtime, but Cooper is not ready to climb into his
mother's pouch and go to sleep until they enjoy some lullabies.
ISBN 978-0-547-40205-5
[1. Bedtime—Fiction. 2. Lullabies—Fiction. 3. Mother and child—Fiction.
4. Kangaroos—Fiction.] I. Munsinger, Lynn, ill. II. Title.
PZ8.3.N92Nig 2013
[E]—dc23
2012041892

Manufactured in China
SCP 10 9 8 7 6 5 4 3 2 1
4500415723

Nighty-Night, Cooper

Written by Laura Numeroff

Illustrated by Lynn Munsinger

Houghton Mifflin Books for Children
Houghton Mifflin Harcourt
BOSTON NEW YORK 2013

Cooper climbed out of his mama's warm pouch.

Dressed in his jammies, he lay on the couch.

His mama sat near him. "I can't sleep," he said.

"Please, can you sing, then I'll go to my bed?"

To the tune of "Rock-a-Bye Baby" . . .

There's a pig sailing

in a small boat

Going so slowly

Floating along

He'll pass a farm

And he'll see some goats

They're fast asleep

They ate all their oats

He'll see the cows
They're taking a snooze

Cats in the sun
Are taking their naps
Sheep in the meadow
Don't make a peep

He'll feel so tired
That he'll fall asleep

"I think that song was very nice.

Now do you know any songs about mice?"

She closed her eyes and thought for a while,

"Yes, my sweet boy," she said with a smile.

To the tune of "The Farmer in the Dell" . . .

A mouse got out of bed

A mouse got out of bed

He drank some milk and brushed his teeth

He is a sleepy-head

A mouse got into bed

A mouse got into bed

He tossed and turned, then fell asleep

And dreamt he found some bread!

"If a mouse got in your bed, what would you do?"

Cooper giggled and his mama laughed, too.

"Please sing the one about the sky that I like.

You sang it the last time we went for a hike!"

To the tune of "Twinkle Twinkle Little Star"...

I see clouds up in the sky

Look for shapes as they pass by
There's a flower and a goat

Over there I spot a boat

I see clouds up in the sky

Look for shapes as they pass by

"Are you getting sleepy?" Mama asked her son.

"A little bit," he said. "Please sing another one?"

"I'll pick a song that will be a surprise.

I'll hold you close, and you close your eyes."

To the tune of "Mary Had a Little Lamb" . . .

PJs are so nice to wear

Nice to wear, nice to wear

PJs are so nice to wear

When you go to bed!

Cooper said, "That's a really good song.

It's not too short and it isn't too long.

How about the one with the daddy and baby bear?

I think they dance and then brush their hair?"

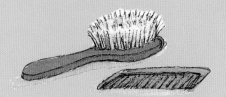

To the tune of "Jingle Bells" . . .

Daddy bear, baby bear

Dancing everywhere

They dance all day
Until it's night
And then they brush their hair!

Oh, *dance all day*
Dance all night

Dance until you doze

Daddy and his baby bear
Can dance up on their toes

"Mama," said Cooper, "I have a song, too!

I learned it in school—can I sing it to you?"

"Yes," said his mama. "It's the last one tonight.

Then you'll go to bed and I'll shut off the light."

Close your eyes, try to sleep

You can start counting sheep

Here comes one, here comes two

I'll keep singing to you

Close your eyes, try to sleep
We can still count the sheep

Close your eyes, all is right
Now I'll kiss you good night

When he was finished, his mama was fast asleep.

Cooper climbed into her pouch and snuggled in deep.

He made himself comfy and laid down his head.

"Good night, my sweet mama. I love you," he said.